Table of Contents

Rourke Educational Media | A Division of Carson Dellosa Education

rourkeeducationalmedia.com

Can you find these words?

larva

prey

tadpoles

wings

Dragonfly

A dragonfly is a flying insect.

A dragonfly **larva** hatches from an egg.

The larva lives in water.

It eats **tadpoles**, fish, and mosquitoes.

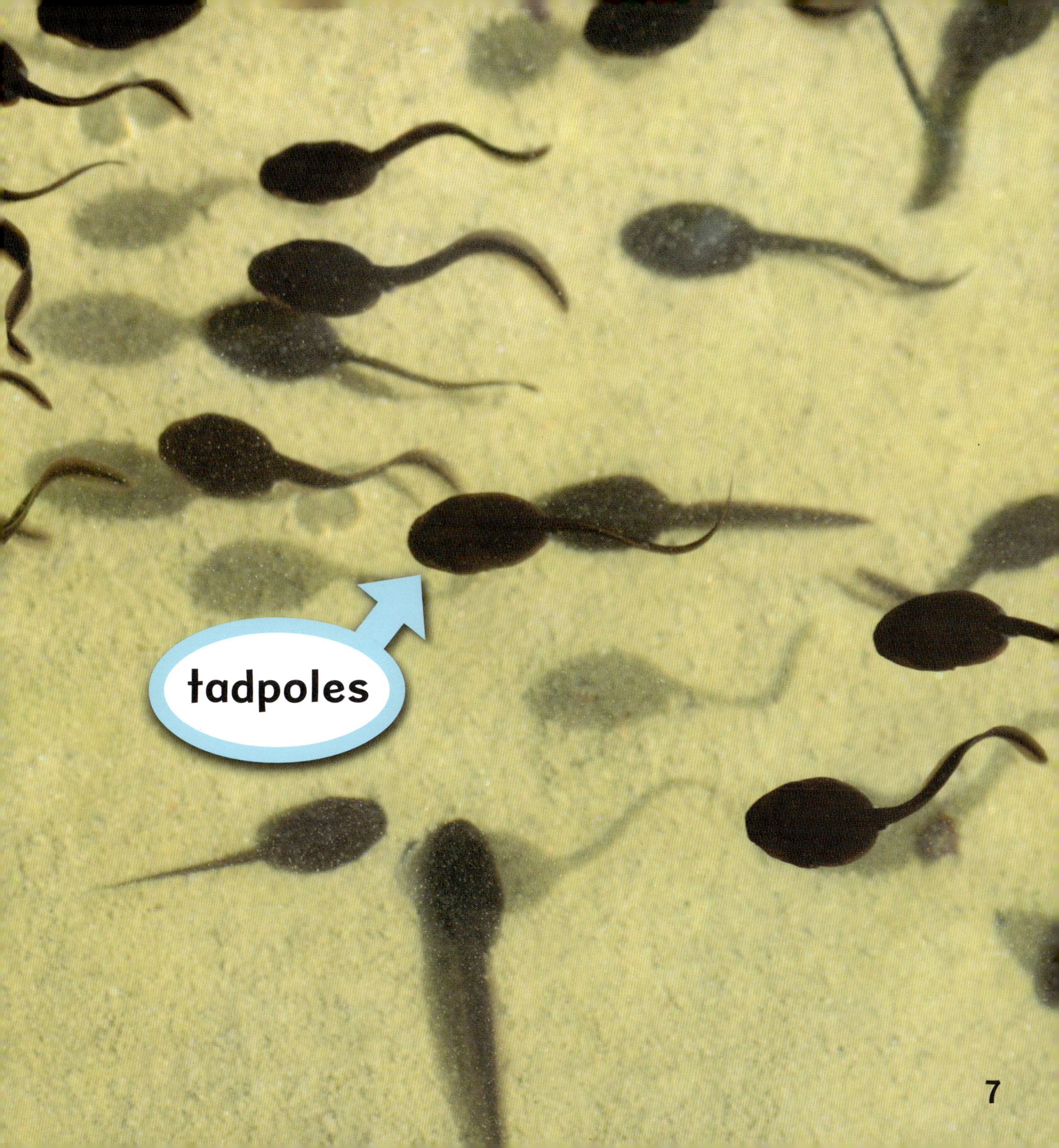
tadpoles

The larva grows up.
Its **wings** pop out!

wings

A dragonfly has big eyes.
It can see all around.

It can see its **prey**.

A dragonfly catches prey with its feet.

Chomp! Yum!

Did you find these words?

A dragonfly **larva** hatches from an egg.

It can see its **prey**.

It eats **tadpoles**, fish, and mosquitoes.

Its **wings** pop out!

Photo Glossary

larva (LAHR-vuh): An insect at the stage of development after hatching from an egg.

prey (pray): An animal that is hunted by another animal for food.

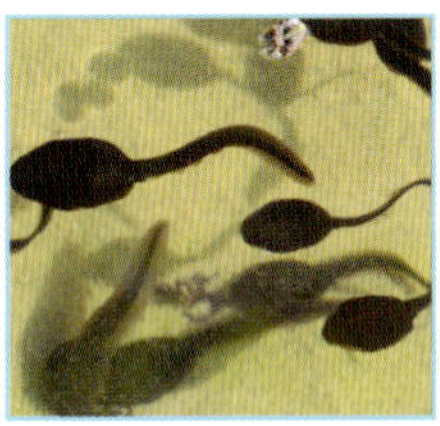

tadpoles (TAD-poles): Young frogs or toads that live in water, breathe through gills, and have long tails but no legs.

wings (wings): Parts of an insect's, bat's, or bird's body that are used to fly.

Index

About the Author

R.E. Robertson is an author and nature lover. His favorite pastimes include reading, cooking, camping, and spending time with his wife, children, and grandchildren.

www.rourkeeducationalmedia.com

PHOTO CREDITS: Cover © Antagain; Pg 2, 11, 14,15 © Awei; Pg 2, 4, 14, 15 © Vitalii Hulai; Pg 2, 6, 14, 15 © kororokerokero; Pg 2, 9, 14,15 © vblinov; Pg 3 © David Havel; Pg 8 © vblinov; Pg 10 © DieterMeyrl; Pg 12 © KRIACHKO OLEKSII; Pg 13 © towlake

Edited by: Keli Sipperley
Cover and interior design by: Kathy Walsh

Library of Congress PCN Data
Dragonfly / R.E. Robertson
(Flying Insects)
ISBN 978-1-73160-580-1 (hard cover)(alk. paper)
ISBN 978-1-73160-439-2 (soft cover)
ISBN 978-1-73160-633-4 (e-Book)
ISBN 978-1-73160-676-1 (ePub)
Library of Congress Control Number: 2018967322

Printed in the United States of America,
North Mankato, Minnesota